THE "FRENCH WRITERS OF CANADA" SERIES

The purpose of this series is to bring to English readers, for the first time, in a uniform and inexpensive format, a selection of outstanding and representative works of fiction by French authors in Canada. Individual titles in the series will range from the most modern work to the classic. Our editors have examined the entire repertory of French fiction in this country to ensure that each book that is selected will reflect important literary and social trends, in addition to having evident aesthetic value.

Current Titles in the Series

Dr. Cotnoir

a novel by
JACQUES FERRON

translated by
Pierre Cloutier

HARVEST HOUSE
Montreal

Advisory Editors
Ben-Zion Shek and Réjean Robidoux,
Department of French,
University of Toronto

For information address Harvest House Ltd.
4795 St. Catherine St. W., Montreal, 215

Printed and bound in Canada.

Designed by Robert Reid.
Cover illustration by Gil. de Cardaillac

The Publishers gratefully acknowledge a publi-
cation grant from The Canada Council.
4

DR. COTNOIR

CHAPTER 1

Three colleagues were present. The others had sent flowers or just a card. The medical profession doesn't die when one of its members does. On the contrary, the loss rejuvenates it. Besides, Cotnoir's death had been something of a relief. Of the three, there was one man too many who had arrived the day before from Temiscouata and if he wasn't unwelcome, he was unexpected. There remained Gérin and myself. I amounted to one man but I was new to the profession and Gérin amounted to half a man since he had only come for the moving of the remains. But he was compelled to go all the way because at the last minute we were told that the three of us would be pall-bearers, along with somebody who came from the suburbs, and Cotnoir's notary. The former was more or less Cotnoir's friend as well as his creditor. He looked liked a fat cat and the notary looked like a rat, tight-lipped and wearing oversized dentures. An odd couple. We weren't enough, though, since the sixth pall-bearer was still missing. We expected Le Royer who had volunteered, or somebody else, but no one came. So the five of us did the job, with the medical men on one side and the businessmen on the other and with the undertakers eagerly helping us along. When the coffin was under the catafalque both groups remained separate. Gérin and the man from Temiscouata sat in the first row of pews, while I sat in the second. We had lost sight of the others. However, during the whole funeral a strange rattling sound could be heard from time to time. The noise came from beyond the catafalque.

"It's the notary," said Gérin to the puzzled man from Temiscouata. Behind us, at the center of a large number of empty pews Mrs. Cotnoir sat alone. Her veil brought out her white hair and the serenity of her face. She had kept her sadness to herself and it dulled her, aged her a little — or perhaps she was just tired out.

In Longueuil, Saint Anthony's is a big church inhabited by saints, angels, apostles and prophets. The heavenly hosts congregate there but long black funeral hangings hid the pageant for the occasion and the heavenly hosts had vanished. A large, earnest crowd could have summoned them back. There was practically no one however. It was a strange funeral. The regular attendants of the church, dry-skinned old men and kinless pious souls, fugitives from the poorhouse, black-clad spinsters, outnumbered us, the participants, and by an extraordinary circumstance they stood there as enemies would. They were seated under the choir loft in the last pews of the nave and looked

8

like judges. At the opposite end of the church, at the heart of the bare chancel, the altar wavered in the warmth of the tapers. White and gold, it looked like a melting honeycake and the priest was nibbling at it, pretending to celebrate the requiem mass. His invocations were all Greek to us. Behind us, however, the court before which no one could plead for the deceased — except his wife who was already appealing to God — was passing judgment on him. The ceremony had been warped and it was a kind of sacrilege. I haven't gotten over it yet. Ten years later it still haunts me.

The service was coming to a close when Le Royer arrived, heralded by a self-consciously stealthy tread which remained heavy-footed because the doctor didn't really insist on remaining unnoticed. He knelt beside me, holding his head in his hands, rapt without further ado. But the cat was out of the bag in no time.

"Well, would you believe it. Nobody came."

Simply the acknowledgment of a fact which surprise soon mitigated, then a certain satisfaction. Le Royer was a tall, handsome man, always sporting English clothes. His patients just adored him. They nursed him more than he did them and he was in very good health. Gérin greeted Le Royer and pointed him out to the man sitting next to him, a lively, ceremonious little old man who seemed very impressed and who bowed, looking the other way as one does in recognition of a celebrity's worth when he isn't an acquaintance.

"Who is he?" asked Le Royer.

I didn't have time to answer. The man was again glancing at Le Royer whom he found fascinating or hadn't quite seen. Le Royer did the same with bowed head, giving him tit-for-tat, then modestly looked elsewhere.

"A colleague?"

"Yes, from Temiscouata."

"Oh!" said Le Royer, striking his most distinguished pose and hanging on. He was not so much inspired by the majesty of his surroundings or due respect for the dead as by that new, that astonishing, that remote thing brought near to him, Temiscouata. The notary wasn't unsettled either by the funeral. His dentures were clattering away simply because he had been scheming and the love of the almighty buck urged him on. The sound — a familiar warning for those who knew him — was his only honesty, they said.

"Why does he do that?" asked the man from Temiscouata.

"To keep from crying," answered Gérin. "Cotnoir was his friend."

The man looked sheepish. He couldn't do quite as much. He had arrived the day before with a fat suitcase. To Mrs. Cotnoir he said:

"I was anxious to get here as you may well understand and I got a ride from the station presto.

10

I am Doctor Antonio Bessette. I'm part Italian and I've been practising for thirty years in St. Eusèbe, Temiscouata. . . . Are you Mrs. Cotnoir?''

"Yes, Doctor."

"It's an awful, awful shame for Léon, for you and for all of us. We were great friends at the university so he probably spoke to you about me. Since then, we hadn't even met. Who would have guessed it at the time? My God, I've thought about him so often. In the summertime it became an obsession. I'd pack my suitcase and then I'd unpack it because I was expecting him and didn't dare leave. The news of his death made me come to a decision. Sick at heart I came, but at least I didn't worry over our paths crossing on the way."

"Yes," the widow said, "he often spoke to me about you."

The man seemed delighted.

"Now, I'll go and drop in at the hotel."

He grabbed his suitcase which was a huge, magnificent thing. Mrs. Cotnoir detained him.

"My husband had no relatives; mine are in France. I'm not expecting anyone. Please stay." He declined the offer, saying he was tired. She insisted. He stayed. While he was settling down in his room she prepared the supper. They ate together solemnly. She smiled, as she usually did, and he sat in the chair of the deceased, slightly

11

bewildered, rather less Italian than on his arrival. When she invited him to come with her and keep vigil over her husband's body after supper, the weariness he had complained of now became a torpor. He went to bed and didn't feel better. An awful pain harassed him so that his eyes were staring wildly. Mrs. Cotnoir called me up and I rushed over. She asked me:

"Have you heard from cousin Emmanuel?"

"No, I haven't."

"Good," she said. And as I was thinking that with all due respect it was a silly excuse for having me come, she added,

"But I didn't have you come here just for that," and went on to explain the case. As soon as Doctor Bessette saw me he cried out:

"Ah, son, you don't know what a bloody awful thing a calculus is!"

And he displayed its consequences for me by a fit. I was wondering whether he would come out of it alive but suddenly the pain went away and he said:

"It's the train. There's nothing worse to shake up the kidneys and rouse the stone slumbering there."

I gave him a shot of morphine.

"I'm sure I'll need another one tomorrow morning before the funeral."

I gave him that second shot and far from being depressed he was brisk and lively.

On the way to church Gérin tried to explain to him that Cotnoir was the victim of unfortunate circumstances. Bessette listened absent-mindedly. His mind was elsewhere. Had he been a horse he would have pranced but he was just jogging along. Then he stopped short with his hand on his mouth.

"Unfortunate? You think so, Doctor?"

"Well, you would think few people cared enough for him to come here at all."

"Yes, of course."

"But it's purely incidental."

"Incidental? I doubt it. Cotnoir had no relatives. Neither did his wife. How can you have a funeral without relatives?"

"Quite a problem," Gérin admitted.

"Do you want to know what I think? Well, when you're dead, you're done for."

"Is that so?"

"Yes, Doctor. If you aren't shoved straight down the hole, if they let you simmer over lampions, if they embalm you, and stuff you, and bake you following the recipes of liturgy, the *cuisine* is for the stomachs of the survivors and I mean the surviving members of the family. There are no professions, or brotherhoods, or ethnic communities in our country. There is only one nation and it's the family!"

"You're absolutely right," said Gérin, raising an eyebrow to glance at the man who continued:

13

"You die and the relatives turn up. But do they want to commemorate? No they don't, Doctor. They come to show off to each other, healthy and fat and well-fed. They grasp the concept of immortality much better than you do, you poor, stiff, lonely, empty corpse. Immortality's for them, the godforsaken bastards, not for you."

"Maybe he has a sense of humour," wondered Gérin.

"If there's a crowd at the funeral, people may say: "He was such a lovable man." But they'll think: "Look: we're VIP's, our town has it made, it pulls the strings." That's a fact and don't try to tell me what the name of the game is. I know a lot more about it than you do."

Mrs. Cotnoir followed the burial procession in the old, black, tall, dented limousine which was in its heyday when her husband bought it during the war and which he had been using for fifteen years. Then, for want of competitors, he'd had a fine practice. It was a rich man's car which he had always driven himself so that the smart alecs could wonder whether he was the chauffeur of Death, the Devil or the Bottle. Time and gossip had given the car an alarming character, and when it drove by it distressed people more than it cheered them up. In the suburbs, they finally called it "the hearse." Mrs. Cotnoir was on the seat which for fifteen years had remained vacant, and an undertaker was driving.

"True, true," said Gérin to his strange companion. "Still, had Cotnoir practised in his own parish he would have drawn more of a crowd today. He was living in Longueuil but didn't have a single patient there. His practice was elsewhere, in suburban slum areas. He liked blue-collar workers."

"A nice man. A very fine man."

"An employer doesn't give his shop workers the day off for them to go and bury a doctor. Living in a big city just isn't the same thing as living in the country, Doctor Bessette."

"Indeed, Doctor, indeed."

"Farmers can lay off work. Anyway, they're bored. Castrate a chicken in church and they'd all come to the service."

Bessette pointed his big nose at Gérin.

"You come from the country, don't you!" And he kept on jogging. The burial procession was coming up main street. It went by the Liquor Commission, the Anglican chapel, city hall, the five banks, the three drugstores, the shops and department stores which made Longueuil a retail trade centre. Just before you come to the church there is the Sisters of Providence hospice. It was one of the finest days of spring, days before the leaves come out, days which make you expect more from the bud than it will, in fact, deliver. The old pensioners of the hospice were facing the

15

street and smiling. Perhaps they thought of living their lives over again. That was when they caught sight of the tall undertaker, the hearse, the truncated, shamefaced funeral procession which could have been theirs, which perhaps was theirs, searching them out. The shock subsided when they found out who was being buried.

We had reached the church and were coming up the steps when the priest loomed out of the main door above us with the choir boys, the tapers, the cross, against the skyscape of the high, multicoloured vault. The coffin was heavy and the deceased wasn't helping himself along. There was a church truck waiting at the top of the steps and we laid our burden on it. We'd barely looked up when the priest began reciting prayers. Gérin nodded from time to time with a solemn look as if he agreed.

"Understand anything?"

"No."

"Neither do I."

A large nose bobbed up between us and Bessette said:

"If God minded our sins, no one could face him."

"That's true," Gérin admitted.

"Do you want me to translate the rest of it?"

"No thanks ... you have quite a memory."

"I know my requiem mass backwards."

Gérin and I looked at each other. A strange

man, Doctor Bessette. A very strange man.

After the moving of the remains we went into the uncannily vacant nave. The last benches only were taken. Had Gérin guessed that the service would be distorted, that the court had moved and was in session not at the front but at the back of the church? With a sweeping gesture, as if to reverse the order of things, he pointed to the confreres, the goody-goodies, the minor stockholders and black spinsters who had been sitting there for years and years perhaps, waiting for their own death. They were absolutely indifferent before Cotnoir's, the death of a doctor who hadn't made a name for himself, a slum celebrity, a disgrace, the shame of the parish, damned from the start.

"The good, decent people! Patients of Doctor Cotnoir to the last man!" Gérin told Bessette.

The man stopped to take a look and Gérin nudged him hard. Surprised, he stared at Gérin who excused himself and took him by the arm. They walked up the centre aisle behind the church truck which the undertaker was pushing, working at it like a cart horse, while the flock of cassocks hurried towards the altar. I was following the businessmen. Behind me, walking with the gait of a young woman and with a simple, undefiant self-confidence, Mrs. Cotnoir stepped forward alone.

CHAPTER 2

While Emmanuel was coming back to town by train, riding the rods round the mountain, Cotnoir who was already home in Longueuil went to bed never to rise again. In the middle of the night, hearing himself gasp he wondered whether he was drunk or sick and suddenly realized that having asked the question, he only had a moment to answer it, which settled the matter. For years, his life had been a burden and had his wife not been there, he would have given it up. Now, he was unexpectedly confronted with the plainness of death, an act which involves you and you only, unwillingly so — and there's the rub — but which becomes your own when you take it upon yourself single-handed. He had enough self-respect not to call out, went Argh! and passed out. But before he did, he had enough time to think that his drunken death would baffle everybody and that help would come too late. He had no time to enjoy the thought. The dying have no sense of humour. They see, they take note and that's it. The instant is too keen for them to elaborate on it, to appraise it, to enjoy it. The cameraman falls, the camera keeps on rolling: a last strip of film which will never be shown. The heart stops and the hair grows and grows. It's refuse. It's irrelevant.

At daybreak the phone rang. Mrs. Cotnoir who had an extension in her room waited for her husband to answer. After five or six rings she thought that he was out and answered the call. Somebody needed a doctor.

"He's out, sir."

"Is he now?! I've called on five, on ten of them. They're all out."

"Listen, give me your phone number and my husband will call you up when he gets back."

"It'll be too late. My wife's dying. Can you hear her?" As the caller presumably pointed the phone towards the back of a room, Mrs. Cotnoir heard a kind of gasping moan.

"That's my wife. Try to understand. Your husband must come right now. He'll save her."

"I'm sorry, sir. I can only say this over again. My husband *is* out."

"I don't believe a word of it." And the man hung up, leaving Mrs. Cotnoir with the telephone in her hand. She had been cut off and could hear the slight humming in the receiver. She hung up, unhappy and puzzled. She couldn't get used to these outbursts which she had had to put up with for years, over and over again, especially as Cotnoir was the only doctor in the area who kept an open line to his clients. The others had an answering service which filtered calls. In case of

an emergency, people tended to call on available
help and to dial Cotnoir's number. He was sometimes absent and his wife weathered out the yells
and insults. An operator's indifference would
have put an end to that but she didn't. She was
sensitive, she couldn't lie, she sympathised with
the callers. When they hung up she was disturbed,
wondering if her husband or she could have done
more. God, a distant echo of her own restlessness,
tenderly concerned over others and never over
Mrs. Cotnoir, didn't reassure her. She only in-
voked him on behalf of her husband.

In the early morning, birds began to sing and
she couldn't get back to sleep. She thought that
they were all starlings. Not a single clear note.
Only the cry of a warbler and the others raising
hell. The man might have been right to doubt
her word. "I can only say this over again, my
husband *is* out." But she hadn't heard her husband going out or coming in and she had been
awake for some time. The buses were moving out
again in the drabness of the sticks. Mrs. Cotnoir
got up and as she was walking up to her husband's
room she heard the gasping moan which she had
heard on the phone, only harsher. She opened the
door. Cotnoir wasn't out. He was lying, his eyes
half shut, foaming at the mouth and black-lipped.

"I was just leaving," answered Gérin. "A
dying woman, or so her husband says. I'll go and

camps with him. Paper mills have their recruiting offices in Saint Paul Street near the Gare du Palais. Lumber camps are full of morons. They make cooks out of them and they make fun of them but nobody ever gets really mean. It's all in a day's work. In a camp a nitwit can find out what human brotherhood really is. That's what Emmanuel needs. It's the only thing which can cure him.''

''What if he doesn't meet any lumberjack?''

''The cops will pick him up. But Québec cops might be more humane than the Montreal police force.''

The dog in the street barked again. Emmanuel loved that.

''Head for Québec, Emmanuel. When you're in Québec head for the logging camps. Got it?''

''Sure.''

Cotnoir got up.

''My husband should be coming home any time now,'' Mrs. Aubertin said. ''I'll talk to him about it.''

''I'll be back this evening.''

''But Emmanuel must be out of the house today.''

''Don't you worry, Mrs. Aubertin. He'll be out of the house.''

''I can't keep him here. Why did they send him back to us? He's insane. They lied. He wasn't cured.''

24

Then Cotnoir left the house, eagerly looking forward to suppertime. He always had supper at home. He described the day's events to his wife. As a matter of fact he spoke of nothing but Emmanuel.

"Yes," she said, "we've got to help the poor man out."

When the priest bent over her dying husband he was gasping and looked like he was done for, already deaf, blind and unconscious, barely strong enough to show that he was petering out fast. The priest said:

"Can you hear me, my son?"

Did Cotnoir hear him? He answered:

"A ticket for Québec."

CHAPTER 3

Winter always spoils towards the end. Its remains in the day's dark corners which escaped the sun were such that a pigeon wouldn't have settled there. The crows had ushered in spring some time ago now. The houses had settled back down into their respective lots on the spot where they stood before the snowfall, respectful of the Chambly county cadastral survey. In the street, the muddy dogs howled.

Towards the end of the afternoon, before the men were home from work and after the children were home from school, in this street which had been laid out the summer before and which still had no name, a kid was loitering, bent over the ditch gutter. He raised his head suddenly, warned by a wild uproar. Cotnoir drove by in his limousine, his face bloated, his neck drawn in, sitting like a monolith. There was no one on the back seat. The kid went home. Anyhow, the sun was setting and the dogs weren't howling any more. Behind the houses, to the south, the marsh was still swarming with activity and things even seemed to be picking up. The frogs' croaking song usually hovered above the swamp during the day but rose in the evening to celebrate the spring moon and to ward off the cold, and then it permeated the suburbs. The marsh, commonly called the "little swamp," was above Coteau Rouge on the boundary line of Saint Hubert and Saint Antoine de Longueuil parish. It had been drained recently.

On the edges of that swamp which was then called the little savannah, the noble Viger and his men ambushed the Red Coats along the Chambly Road and set off the revolt of 1837. The Red Coats ran like dogs. Viger had the tip of one thumb cut off. A little blood, the rustling of the bulrushes, the magnificence of autumn, all on an imaginary line linking Mount Royal to St. Bruno.

The kid told his mother what he had seen. She went to the window and drew the curtains aside slightly. "The hearse" was parked in front of the Aubertin home.

"What's the problem?" wondered Cotnoir as he climbed down from the tall car. On the phone a neighbour had clamoured for an emergency visit. He didn't know anything more as she had hung up.

"A cut and they lost their heads at the sight of blood? No, the Aubertins don't have any boys. A fainting fit?"

Cotnoir only had to go in to find out. But he didn't hurry, guessing, wondering, trying to imagine what had happened so as to pull himself together in the meantime.

"Considering the number of women in the house," he thought "— one mother and six daughters — that should be three fainting fits: a major fit and two minor ones which leaves four girls available, one for cold compresses, the others rubbing down the hands and forearms of the girls who are out cold, with coarse salt. That's why no one is watching out for me and asking me to come on in. They're all busy in there."

But then, should he come in by the front or the back door, he wondered? Cotnoir was short of breath and walked with measured tread. He had to, especially when he had a hangover and then he spared himself as many steps as he could. It was shorter to come in by the front door. But it was blocked up during the winter and he would have found it shut, so he walked round the house to the back.

Bulrushes on the edge of the yard. In the background, winter's rubbish was heaped around a car frame. The sight reminded him of the forgotten crows beyond the walls and partitions of a day's thousand sectioned spaces, the crows which could be seen that very morning at sunrise, here and there, on the clotheslines of the sleeping suburb and which were so remote now.

"Springtime in the junkyard. Dust all over soon. Jesus Christ."

If the end of the day made him fidgety, rest-

"Maybe your wife should replace her statue with a Hollywood pin-up while there's still time. Make it a sexy one."

But the coal-man hunched his shoulders. A son. Why should he have a son? He didn't even consider it. He just adored his daughters, he was defenceless, infatuated, the very image of potent fatherhood, immensely satisfied.

His house had long stood alone, far from the suburbs, on the edge of the little swamp, a five-minute walk from the Chambly Road. He'd built it out of jealousy because he was a coal-man and his wife was quite young and fair. He thought, not unjustifiably, that he could have her more as his very own far from the crowd, and she found it quite inconvenient. In the summer the bush hemmed the house in and it looked out on nothing but the swamp. At least in winter when the trees stood out brown against the snow the young woman could catch sight of the houses of Coteau Rouge, the city smog, Mount Royal beyond the bushes which had shed their leaves. If she could only have surrounded herself with the photographs of pin-ups and skyscrapers she liked! But her husband chose the pictures, adding to the undergrowth of the forests, the swamps of the lakes and rivers, the confinement of the mountains, as if leaving her alone for days on end with a moose who didn't take his eyes off her wasn't bad enough.

34

Then the years passed, the children were born and the suburb gradually crept closer. Finally a street stretched from the house to Chambly Road. However, Aubertin was now less concerned over his wife than over his daughters. He had bought a parakeet for each and a large bird cage where the six of them chattered away. These birds had given the house a kind of airy, naive, ludicrous cheerfulness. The coal-man was no longer at odds with the world or society. On the contrary, he thought of running for the municipal council. Still, there were women in it, swarms of them, his daughters he wanted to impress. He had thrown off the jealous man, the lone wolf he had been. Because he had settled down first in the area he thought of himself as a pioneer, a founding father, and expected to have a street named after him. He even bought a hat though he had never worn one. One day, he received an official letter wherein it was written that society needed him. It didn't surprise Aubertin. He had been expecting it for some time now. He put on his hat and headed triumphantly for the skyscrapers of Montreal.

A lady whose glasses were more prominent than her tits greeted him. Her voice sounded like a loudspeaker and the convincing robot said:

"Mr. Aubertin, you are a dependable citizen and a landed proprietor. Society rests on your

35

its aid and to ease the strain now exerted upon it.''

Aubertin answered:

''I couldn't agree with you more, ma'am.''

Like a baboon looking up, ready to climb a mast, he expected her to rise to lofty considerations of governments, ministers and slush funds. The baboon never got off the ground. The woman began an ominous *exposé* on the family and duty towards one's relatives. In fact, saying ''Isn't that so, Mr. Aubertin,'' she had him stuck with a cousin he hadn't seen for ten years, cousin Emmanuel then residing in the Bordeaux loony-bin for publicly taking his pants down on a balcony not only to exhibit himself but to piss upon the local residents.

''Don't you worry, Mr. Aubertin, he has been treated and he is cured. All he needs is someone who can help him readapt to the outside world. We're only asking you to look after him for one or two weeks.''

Mr. Aubertin must have been quite obviously unhappy. The robot took off its glasses and came closer to him. Insubstantial tits. Why not take them off too?

''Come now, you mustn't do this reluctantly.''

On second thought, she should keep them on. Made her look candid.

''I'm willing enough.''

That's what he told her but once out of the office he could have bitten his tongue, and he

36

swore he wouldn't even think about politics ever again. A man of his word, he then went and picked up cousin Emmanuel. The poor thing was confused, quivering, completely bewildered although he kept a straight face. Because it was a cold day and he didn't have a hat, Aubertin handed Emmanuel his municipal magistrate's hat. He put it on solemnly and they both headed for home. Aubertin looked at no one. Emmanuel was greeting passers-by behind his back.

handed him over to a bunch of hangmen. I saw a couple of them. They all seemed bored. They were always checking what time it was and time in there is like the clock of hell stopped dead.

"These guys are like devils, ma. When they're bored they get really mean. I'm telling you, all the prison guards, the policemen, the orderlies I saw in there seemed to be afraid their watch was going to stop. And they handed my cousin over to them!

"The judge said 'This boy should be treated' and handed him over to the executioner. Some judge he was. The hangmen got to work on Emmanuel and look at the results. A pretty thorough job. If they had gotten their hands on you you'd be just like him, on the lookout with your ears perked, terrified by anything you hear except the sound of water, tap water pouring away. He was a good guy, not too smart, but helpful. He got laughed at but he was no fool. He kept his job as a poultry plucker for twenty years until the day when his boss died. He wasn't an idiot, he just played the fool and that's different. It was an act. He might have been cut out for it but he was no fool. Being dumb was a stunt and everybody loved it and asked for more and Emmanuel did his stuff and obliged them. He had no family. He was looking for someone who would adopt him that way. When his boss died, perhaps the new man wasn't too patient, and Emmanuel thought he couldn't be laid off after twenty years of service. They couldn't stand each other and you can guess who took off. Then he went from one tavern to the other. And why did they put him in the clink? He must have been down and out. Don't tell the kids, but he bet that he would piss on people from a balcony. He wasn't lucky on that bet and won a trip to the nut-house, a hell darker than the good God's own. The poor guy had never hurt a living soul. He was always trying to oblige. The day he walked into that prison he was really innocent and it wasn't an act or a stunt either. Pissing on those people. They didn't deserve it for allowing men to be locked up? Anyway, ma, Em-manuel is our guest. We'll help him off to a new start. Have him clean the yard. That'll keep him busy and when the weather is nice, we'll sow grass up to the edge of the bulrushes.''

This was the enlightening speech which Auber-tin delivered before his wife who didn't feel that happy about the project because of the madman of course, but also because her husband was putting his heart and soul into it and transforming the whole thing into an adventure. As to his com-passion, compassion is quite prevalent among the common people. A hard life and the nerve it calls for demand it. Aubertin wasn't without mis-givings either. Why should he save a cousin he hardly knew? Because he had given his word to a woman he didn't know either, because he hated the bloody system, because he felt compassionate? Yes. But all of this was less important than his temperamental, unpredictable personality, its ever latent capacity for lack of foresight which kept drama within its scope and allowed him to bear with society, the ant-hill. Aubertin was improvising and this disturbed him, coming as it did from a family man and a landed proprietor. He didn't know how to wrap the whole thing up. Emmanuel's future was at stake, of course, but it was also a question of the reaction of a small community to the misfortune of one man. What would that reaction be? Can you cure bad luck or is it contagious? Can't anything just leak out of this world? He would save Emmanuel but at whose expense? It so happened that in the group which Aubertin was putting in jeopardy there were six girls and one cageful of birds. The apple of his eye was at stake. He wasn't at all confident, so that when he returned from work on the next day and learned that the cousin had begun to take notice of the parakeets, he was frankly apprehensive.

"Are they nice birds, Emmanuel?"

"Sure."

"Tell me now, wouldn't you sometimes feel like plucking them by any chance?"

Emmanuel glanced at his cousins.

"... Plucking them, like you did to the hens for so long."

Emmanuel answered:

"Sure."

He regretted that remark. Aubertin burst out:

"Now you listen here. You ever touch those birds and I'll wipe the floor with you."

Emmanuel was so terrified that he thought the moose had spoken. He locked himself up in the bathroom and the tap began to run again. Meanwhile, the neighbour who chattered like a magpie and was a self-important pest: an inquisitive, malicious, serviceable and even irreplaceable person, came snooping around for news. Aubertin didn't stand and his face was still smeared with coal. He asked her if she couldn't look after this cousin of his. She had no children. She was shrewd, smart.

"I can't do it. My husband's much too jealous."

"But how could he be jealous of a village innocent?"

"Emmanuel isn't as innocent as all that."

The coal-man didn't labour the point, but still, he wanted to find out what she would have done in his place.

"I would have left your cousin where he was."

"I think that's a heartless thing to say."

And he stood up, probably to show that *he* wasn't heartless.

"Maybe I'm callous but you don't have any brains and I·can prove it. You're stuck with that madman and you just wanted to hand him over

43

to me so he could pluck me alive.''

''I would say that was done a long time ago.''

The neighbour was her friend and adviser and Mrs. Aubertin intervened. But her friend, who was thin when she would have liked to be a plump little dairy maid and who looked like a plucked bird without her clothes, was even more offended because Aubertin knew what he was talking about. She was on the verge of saying things which would have been offensive to all present and Aubertin could see it coming.

''Come on now, let's not lose our temper.''

As she said, ''Why don't you go and wash up!'' she tried to open the bathroom door which was locked from within. She began to laugh.

''Well, we still have the swamp,'' she said and went out, leaving the rather miserable coal-man with his dirty face and his equally tarnished soul.

CHAPTER 6

When he stayed at the house of a so-called late college or university friend, Doctor Bessette whose real name was Bezeau, and who came from Abitibi not Temiscouata, usually got up early. Death always upsets a household. A clever man can be on the prowl for a little money, some jewelry, enough to live on between two funerals. The early morning was a very suitable time for a rip-off.

Bezeau didn't alter his habits. He came down from his room at about six. In the living room two little nuns were keeping vigil over Cotnoir's body. Seeing them didn't distress him. On the contrary. Had they been relatives they would have heard him come down and found an occasion to evade the call of duty, but they didn't even budge. He took advantage of this and went through their large black cloaks which were hanging near the door. He found a few coins given them for their good works, took his rightful share and did the same with a money box which he found in one of the kitchen cupboards. Then he cooked himself a good breakfast. He had enough time to go into his colleague's office while the water was heating and came back with a vial of demerol and twenty-two morphine ampules. The loot was beyond his expectations and he went up quickly to tuck it away in his large suitcase. He came back down at once and enjoyed his breakfast.

A few minutes later Mrs. Cotnoir came down. She recited a short prayer with the nuns and dismissed them. They put on their large black cloaks and left. Coming into the kitchen she jumped with fright.

"You hadn't noticed the smell of the coffee?"

"So you're up."

"Your breakfast is ready, Mrs. Cotnoir. Please sit down and eat."

He seemed so pleased with the meal he had prepared that she sat down although she wasn't hungry at all. He served her and said:

"Eat, you need it. Meanwhile I'll go and keep our poor friend company."

When he was in the presence of the corpse he couldn't help crying. A vial of demerol and twenty-two ampules of morphine. He was a millionaire. He had enough for a week at least. To think he hadn't believed that Cotnoir was also an addict. What's more, he had raked up about twenty dollars, the price of a ticket for New England if a colleague ever died there, that is a colleague from Laval or Montreal, because as far as the others were concerned….There had been an unfortunate incident. Coming to Boston for the funeral of a doctor called Arthur Maheu, he broke out into his "It's an awful shame for Arthur" routine and people stared at him. No one in the house spoke French and he didn't know a word of English. He found out that Maheu belonged to a vintage American family and had studied at the University of Vermont. After this setback, he decided to limit his rounds to Laval and Montreal graduates only.

His neck drawn in, his little mustache growing out of his nose like a closely knit lump, Cotnoir just didn't seem to be there, oddly enough. Bessette did not recognize him at all and he wasn't surprised. What intrigued him was his lack of relatives.

"You poor man, how could you be godforsaken with that boozer's face?"

It was puzzling.

"You weren't born on the wrong side of the tracks. You had enough dough to get an education and become a doctor. How did your parents go about drilling a hole in the landscape and leaving you fatherless on the other side? Didn't people have car accidents or drown when you were a kid?"

Bessette slapped himself on the forehead. He had it. Influenza. Cotnoir's French wife wasn't much of a problem. His diploma in hand, the little doctor, bull-necked, and equally determined, his mustache beginning to grow out of his nose, had headed for fair France to finish his education there. It was quite natural that he should not return alone. An orphan himself, he brought back an orphan girl. They had had no children because they feared to give birth to orphans, what else?

This is what Bessette was thinking about as he knelt on the prayer stool where one of the little nuns had knelt. But these considerations inadvertently dried up his tears and he regretted it. He wasn't going to let good old Cotnoir, his university days' buddy fade away without displaying genuine grief. He thought about the morphine again. Twenty-two ampules, not to mention the demerol. And thank God the tears welled back into his eyes. To keep them coming he went from the morphine and the security it provided him to thoughts of his wife and his thirty years of honest practice in Abitibi. The tears kept on coming somehow or other. From time to time he blew his nose, making it sound like a trumpet call. Finally Mrs. Cotnoir came in. He was quite glad though he seemed annoyed at having betrayed his grief. He wiped his eyes briskly and pulled himself together like an old coquette. The widow knelt on the prayer stool next to his. She looked at her husband for a long time and didn't seem to recognize him either. Did Bessette understand the cause of her misery? He said:

"You shouldn't look for him where he no

longer exists. From now on he lives within you.''

He hadn't thought it up himself but the words were appropriate. Roaming from one funeral to another the man had learned to get his message across.

''Thank you,'' said the widow, closing her eyes. Like people do in church when speaking to each other, without moving he whispered:

''Thank *you* for not abandoning him.''

''Why should I have done that?''

''You could have done what everybody does, deliver him into the venal hand of the undertaker.''

''This is a large house. It was more convenient for me to keep him here.''

''In a funeral home he would have been alone twelve hours a day at the mercy of the rats.''

''I'm afraid that is an overstatement.''

''Well, I get worked up over the whole issue but a belief in God does imply an affectionate devotion for the dead, you know what I mean?''

''Yes, and I agree.''

''The fact of the matter is there's precious little of it left. A man dies and he is promptly shipped to people who know and care as much about religion as a butcher does. In the old days they used to call on the services of an undertaker but there was always a relative keeping an eye on him. They wouldn't let the body out of their sight from the moment of death until the burial. Now, we

49

hand the departed over to complete strangers. They lie in state in these hideous temples all alone from ten in the evening to ten in the morning.

"Yes," she said, "I know."

"And just who manages the temples? A businessman, that's who. Can't you see that there's a new, barbaric and inhuman religion in the making whose Pope will be a Grand Undertaker?"

"Doctor, you're exaggerating. Construction styles have changed. Now private homes are too small for the dead to lie in state there."

"But construction styles are the most symptomatic element of a culture. Besides, if private homes are too small, dedicated individuals, priests, monks or nuns should substitute for the next of kin."

Mrs. Cotnoir didn't answer and Bessette, eating his heart out, didn't dare distrub her again. Soon the undertakers came to prepare the funeral.

"Look at them," he said, "fat, ruddy, healthy. A mid-Victorian put-on if I ever saw one."

Mrs. Cotnoir got up to leave.

"I hate their guts," Bessette said.

He followed her and they went into the kitchen. That's where I caught up with them. I had brought my medical bag.

"Ah, my friend in need." Without another word he motioned me to lead on and we both went up to his room where he took off his jacket.

"Did you sleep well?"

"Not really."

"What about the pain?"

"Dull but still there. You've got it cornered all right and it might make a comeback, so you get in there and assassinate the bitch."

He rolled up his sleeve and stretched out his arm. The day before, I'd given him his shots in the backside and hadn't noticed anything special but his arm was riddled with little haematoid spots which showed that he'd had a couple. Under the skin the muscle was indurated. I didn't know what to do. Bessette was staring me down with impertinent, cunning little eyes.

"Poor old arm of mine," he said. "Shot up, isn't it?"

"Yes, it certainly is."

"A severe case of anemia. Three calf-liver injections a day, that's what saved me."

I gave him his morphine. He rolled down his sleeve and put his jacket back on.

"Now be honest, son, you did think I was an addict, didn't you?"

"I did," I said with embarrassment.

"Well, let me tell you how I couldn't become one even if I wanted to. It's still early so have a seat and listen to this."

I thought of Mrs. Cotnoir. I wanted to hear him out but worried over her loneliness even more.

"Come on now, sit down."

Through the bedroom door which had remained open I saw Gérin who was coming in, standing at the foot of the stairs. I sat and, taking things easy, Doctor Bessette said:

"You never knew Doctor Antoine Bezeau who was an Abitibi homesteader, did you? He was Cotnoir's colleague and mine, not a terribly smart man, hard working, clean living and stone broke of course. He got his Doctorate when Cotnoir sailed happily for Europe and he settled down in La Flèche, a small village, nothing but clay in the subsoil, no mines, strictly farming country. There he worked his head off, bought himself a house and three years later married the village schoolmarm. They were both in their thirties and both virgins. You can see it from here. Well, they were madly in love — funny that — had a son and a daughter and still had it bad. They weren't rich. Bezeau nursed his patients in a puny, apprehensive, scrupulous sort of way which no one trusted, not even himself.

"He was an honest man."

"He was paid accordingly. He got his children educated somehow. His son became an engineer and settled down in Ontario where he married an Irish girl. His daughter became a nun. He gradually lost touch with both but didn't mind it that much because his wife was still around. However, one day she fell sick and the Amos surgeons couldn't do a thing for her. She was a termi-

52

nal case and they sent her back home after a little radium therapy. She survived for a year. Morphine did her a lot of good. The problem was that she had gotten into the habit of sharing anything she enjoyed with her husband who was also her doctor and after she'd had her shots she couldn't help asking him to have one too. He always refused but she threatened him with turning down the only comfort she had left. She was emaciated and pitiful and he had to give in. From then on when he gave her an injection he gave himself one too. He lay down beside her; she held his hand and they would go on these trips together. A strange, a very strange honeymoon.

"After his wife's death he kept on doing it, neglecting his practice and attracting the attention of the narcotics squad. Soon he was homeless, penniless and didn't have any morphine left. Where could he go? To his son's home? They only spoke English there and he spoke nothing but French. Suicide. How would he go about it? He was in a tight spot but an innocuous bit of news solved the problem. The death of a colleague he hadn't seen for thirty-five years. Didn't even remember what he looked like. And where had the man died? Rimouski, a town he'd never even seen. Who cares.

"He borrowed the price of his ticket from his daughter's convent and away he went in spite of his age, his conscience, in spite of everything.

He was happy-go-lucky and roaming about from one funeral to the other all over the country. He'd been a fool but he became clever, very clever."

Bessette stared at me with little insolent eyes.

"Say, you might be wondering why Doctor Bezeau isn't here?"

"Yes, that's right," I ventured to say, "I might be."

"He's dead, son, and nobody ever found out, nobody ever will."

Saying that, he showed me the door and I went out.

CHAPTER 7

When Aubertin came home that evening he found his wife speechless, his daughters soberly pottering about, the parakeets alert but keeping up a sardonic front. He thought that the adventure was over and that Emmanuel was no longer in the house. The tap wasn't running any more. There was no trace of the disturbance which the poor man had brought about.

The coal-man almost suspected that Emmanuel had been sent away without his consent but he saw him sprawling on the couch, sleeping in the protective shadow of the moose. His authority was confirmed and he took advantage of the fact that the bathroom was available to wash up. Then he dressed in his Sunday best because the occasion called for it and was so good as to sit down to dinner.

"What happened?" he said.

His wife who hadn't uttered a word and who was just waiting for her cue said:

"What was bound to happen, what else. You were taken in. Your cousin wasn't back to normal. He did something even worse than the first time. The first time he made a bet, not a very

55

smart thing to do but it gave him a reason for doing it. This time he went ahead and did it for no earthly reason, whammo, out of a blue sky like a real lunatic. I was shocked, I was. Not because of his poor, lean, hairy bum but because what he did showed just how much brains he had. Anyway I don't want to have him around the house."

"All right, he'll go."

"When?"

"Tomorrow if you want him to."

"He's leaving tonight. I've arranged it."

Aubertin hadn't dressed to go to bed in his Sunday best. He also wanted to deal with the matter of his cousin's presence, to do it that very evening, but he wanted to do it his way. He frowned when he learned that it had been settled behind his back, found the supper not well prepared, just awful. Papa-moose shoved his plate back and enquired in a high and mighty voice:

"Just what's been arranged without my knowing it?"

The bedroom statue covered up its chest. The little game of the daggers and the bull's eye heart was over. The big show under the big top was over. He'd put his foot in it. A real girl with good, round breasts came back at him while the delighted parakeets were chuckling away.

"If you think we were going to sit there and idolize you know what, waiting until you came in

56

in your own good time, you're dead wrong. We kept you in mind though. I remembered what you found out at the nut house. I'm no cow even if I don't write speeches for the municipal council. And I don't think anyone should get a raw deal because I want us to be happy so I kept the neighbour from calling the police."

Aubertin brightened up. He was subdued, no longer wearing any antlers, almost like a little boy.

"What did you do?"

"I wasn't in my right mind and she wasn't either. She was really flying off the handle and that helped me keep a cool head. Then I thought about asking Cotnoir to come over. She rushed for the phone, cried out for help and he came. Before he did, Emmanuel, whose bum was all wet, had enough time to pull his pants back on."

"His bum was wet?"

"Well, she'd told the girls to shut their eyes but they didn't listen to her. Anyway Linda kept hers wide open and splashed a glass of water up his ass. Then when Cotnoir came in, things had settled down some."

"Except for the neighbour."

"Except for the neighbour but he took no account of her. Besides, he was a little drunk as usual. He grabbed Emmanuel by the hair to look at his face. He's a good judge of character. He thought what you thought, that Emmanuel was a nice guy. She didn't seem to agree, so he told her we all take our pants off some time or other and that made the girls laugh. He even said he knew some people who did it more often than they ought to. She must have figured he was referring to her and stiffened up. Thanks to Cotnoir everyone but she thought the whole thing was pretty funny. If he'd kept it up, in the long run we would have thought that nothing at all had happened and that we'd been seeing things. I had to remind him of a few facts. A madman's a madman and a home just isn't a loony-bin. He agreed with me and I told him about my decision.''

"Your decision?"

"I decided Emmanuel would go and get cured somewhere else but wouldn't be handed over to the cops. So, he thought there was only one way of doing it, getting him on tonight's train for Québec. His scheme is pretty complicated. After the trip to Québec I can't figure it out, but he'll be back later after his rounds and he'll explain it to you.''

Aubertin felt his appetite coming back and had a second helping. This time he liked the food. It was the same stew but served by a different woman. He couldn't get over it. He was eating with deliberate leisureliness, trying to imitate the beautiful people who attend to their needs so elegantly that you would think they had none and ate simply for the sheer gracefulness of the gesture. Why did he stage this little comedy when he had just been outmanoeuvred? Did he guess that his attempt wasn't defeated because he was, that others would carry on where he left off, that human solidarity was involved? Perhaps. Anyhow, he could see that something had been altered in the world, and he vaguely thought he could be credited with having initiated it.

CHAPTER 8

When the undertakers had shut the coffin, they stripped the living room of its flowers and picked up their things, props, plaster-works, ornaments. They worked slowly but dextrously: they were cautious and wanted to get it over with. Bessette was observing them from the top of the tall staircase and they watched out for him like shifty-eyed fowl. They became much better undertakers. One of them even began to do obeisances each time he passed before the coffin and the others soon imitated him. They were *so* respectful. The tall undertaker supervised the work with the look of a madam keeping a close eye on her prostitutes parading before a very old and very solemn client. From time to time, he glanced up the staircase to see through the old man and find out what his tastes were but Bessette was an old roué and didn't turn a hair, probably waiting until he could find among these subordinates the whore of his choice.

The house's ground plan was symmetrical. I was in the dining room which was the living room's counterpart on the opposite side. The doors of both faced each other across the lobby where the staircase came down. There was a passageway alongside it leading to the back of the house. It was a big middle-class home built at the end of the last century when large amounts of available lumber and ridiculously low salaries gave people who were moderately well off the opportunity of owning quite a house. A large mirror hung on the wall of the passageway. Thanks to it, from the dining room I could catch a glimpse of Bessette observing the scene. I didn't take my eyes off him. He still puzzled me although I'd understood just who he was. I was still hovering between admiration and pity and didn't know which would win out. The astonishing transformation of the poor country doctor into a con-man fascinated me, especially when I considered the age at which the change had been effected.

My attention was taken off him by the arrival of old Mr. Sauviat. I knew him by sight and by reputation. He was quite a character, he lived in the suburbs and astonishingly enough, beneath a thick head of whitened red hair he was as moody as an adolescent — a much more enlightened man for all that. He had dabbled in holy orders and never quite recovered concerning his relationship with women. Simply hadn't been able to get back in touch. They were as alien to him as insects. But human nature had retaliated with this little fairy he had in his blood. She was even more unexpected since the old man wasn't exactly a babe-in-arms. He hung out on the premises of the Crown Realty and Duplessis Investment Company, wheeling and dealing and living alone in his office like a fat cat in a hole. He rarely came out of it but his influence could be felt everywhere. He had his pimps, informers, protégés and homos and besides his victims there were a number of clients known as "the royal family" — an offbeat nickname. *He* was George V because he resembled Edward VII. He didn't mind that at all and was clownishly proud of it. Sauviat was vain but he was too shrewd, too mischievous not to be the first to make fun of this likeness though he cultivated it carefully. I knew that Cotnoir had seen a good deal of him and that they were on friendly terms.

I wasn't too surprised to see him walk in. He was, though. He was astonished to be out of his sordid kingdom and to find himself powerless, disarmed, obsequious, quivering like an old Breton friar out of his community. Coming in he went and shook hands with a pint-sized undertaker who shook hands with him inadvertently and stood there gaping. Then Sauviat was totally confused. He had obviously put his foot in it but instead of cutting the incident short, the poor man felt the fairy blushing within and his hair going wild with panic. He didn't let the hand go, he held it, pumped it and didn't stop until finally he did let go, almost choking, and managed to say: "Thank you my good man," as if the little undertaker had expressed his heartfelt sympathy. Anyhow the tall undertaker was coming to the rescue of his assistant and with a considerate respect which fooled no one brought the old man, in a sweat and mopping his brow, to me. That must have kept his hands full because he forgot to shake mine. And how was Mr. Sauviat, I asked.

"Yes, yes. Very well, very well indeed," he said, wiping his eyes now, stirred by his own sensitiveness, secure behind his handkerchief, trying to look me over because he didn't know just who I was and was trying to guess, still too upset to simply ask.

I went back to the mirror. Bessette was no longer on the staircase landing. Just then, a hand settled on my shoulder and I jumped. It was him.

"Son, why don't you introduce me to this gentleman I've never had the pleasure to meet."

I did and the two cronies greeted each other solemnly. Then Bessette said:

"The odds are you're a businessman and you like to deal in real estate, am I right?"

Sauviat who was recovering quickly answered.

"I can see that you are quite a diagnostician. I'm just a nobody, really, and wouldn't even claim to be half as good a judge of character as you are. But if I may, I would say that you are not just a medical man."

64

"Well, I would. I practise in St. Eusèbe de Temiscouata. How can you be anything but 'just a medical man' when you're doing that?"

"I'm sorry. I meant to say that you had other interests besides medicine. I wouldn't be surprised if you were interested in the stock market, more particularly mining stocks."

"There, you've found me out. But not any old stocks, mind you. Copper mines and copper mines only! Mr. Sauviat, copper mine stocks are the best buy in the world."

Sauviat, a man who was aware of better ore deposits, agreed politely. Meanwhile the hearse had arrived. You could catch sight of it through the window near which we stood. It was an excellent excuse for changing the subject of the conversation as copper had a hollow ring to it. However, I had found Doctor Bessette's profession of his faith quite interesting. When I heard him repeat it to Gérin, not making much more of a hit than the first time because Gérin who was already nibbling away at something else couldn't be lured, I understood that it was a swindler's gimmick. I also admired the speed with which he could probe a man and withdraw when greediness wasn't aroused. Copper then seemed to be an obsession among the other obsessions of a paradoxical and baffling individual from whom the most absurd foolishness could be expected. Pointing to the hearse he said:

"Gentlemen, at least horses were honest."

And went on:

"In any case, they were preferable to the rats which now haunt funeral homes. Enormous rats! Mind you, they're well fed."

"Oh, now Doctor!" Sauviat chuckled.

"When the rats get big enough they simply turn them into undertakers. Things tend to have this protean quality about them in funeral homes. Do you know the story of the three heads? Three bodies were lying in state. The first wore a navy blue suit, the others grey ones. The suits were very prosaic things, you had a front, two sleeves and no back. As to the pants there just weren't any. The dead of our generation will be nice looking indeed at the last judgment."

"Now, now, Doctor."

"Well, the widow of the first man came up, took a look at her husband and decided she'd rather have him wearing grey. The undertaker told her: "Fine, come back in ten minutes." She did and her husband was wearing the grey suit but all things considered, she thought he looked nicer with the blue one. "Right," said the undertaker. "Come back in ten minutes." She miscalculated and came back in five but the job was already done. She apologized and marvelled at the efficiency of the man. He shrugged. He had only been switching the heads."

The old boy was chuckling away, amazed at

this cold, cold cynicism. He had forgotten his embarrassment and no longer regretted having stepped out of role for once, like an old Breton friar who has lived through hard times and runs into a bishop who is the soul of meek ingenuousness. He was blissfully unaware of the notary's arrival. The notary who had grown accustomed to more consideration was shocked.

"Speaking of heads," the bishop was saying, "do you remember the case of the decapitated corpse?"

"Absolutely. The head is still missing as well as both hands. The police haven't found them yet. Mind you, they found the feet."

"You have a fine memory, let me tell you. Now, what does an undertaker need to prepare a dead man for his last parade?"

"His corpse I guess."

"You're being extravagant, Mr. Sauviat. The head and both hands pinned to a dummy will do the job."

"What about the body?"

"You can take it to the municipal garbage dump. You can eat it. Well, have you figured it out? That wasn't murder. It was an undertaker's practical joke."

"Oh, doctor, doctor," chuckled Sauviat, translated into the seventh heaven.

Someone coughed. It was the big undertaker who respectfully asked if he could join us. He hadn't timed it right. Bessette stared at him with his small, impudent eyes. That didn't bother him at all. He had grown accustomed to all kinds of faces.

"Isn't it too bad that so few people came," he said baldly. Did Sauviat remember that he was George V? He breathed in hard.

"Sir," he answered, "only quality matters," and he remained inflated. Fortunately Mrs. Cotnoir came in from the back of the house escorted by Gérin. Sauviat dropped a low, an astonishing, an endless curtsy. A queen couldn't have been made more welcome. It made him blush. The notary slapped him on the back.

"Come on, now's the time to speak to her." And he rushed towards her followed by Sauviat who was deflated and pale. They caught her in the hall and Gérin joined us. Then Bessette tried out his copper routine on him but he just wouldn't touch the stuff.

"Doctor Gérin is too much of a patriot to be concerned with the baser metals," I said gravely.

"Is he?" said Bessette. "Well, so am I. Don't speak a word of English. Are you a patriot like me?"

"More or less," answered Gérin.

"I respect you for that. Very few people are now. Do you know that in a couple of years nobody will be able to afford it?"

"Dead right," said the undertaker in English.

"Doctor, you're a gentleman!"

Sauviat and the notary didn't let Mrs. Cotnoir be. I didn't like it. Did they have anything that important to tell her? Gérin answered that they were probably trying to find out her plans for the future.

"She'll return to France," he said.

"They'll swindle her."

"No. They're old enough to require our services."

"Do you mean they'll play it straight because they're afraid of getting killed?"

The big undertaker seemed worried.

"Yes," Gérin answered.

"Anyway, I'd murder both willingly."

Bessette put his hand on my shoulder.

"Now, there's a fine little doctor for you."

The undertaker, snapping out of his daydream, looked at his watch. We were late. Le Royer hadn't arrived yet. Still, he had promised he would be there.

"By the way," Gérin said to Bessette, "he's the kind of man who takes an interest in copper mining stocks."

And we walked out following the coffin.

CHAPTER 9

Crows are always on the lookout. When the pace of city life slackens they come nearer, speaking to each other above it in quick shrieks. The pace always slackens at dawn, a time when night turns pale, when the unhappy people who haven't been able to sleep hear them. But the crows say to each other:

''Today isn't the day,'' and move off while the city awakes. Every morning they return, waiting for the day when the city will not awake. Then they will swoop in through the windows. The eyeball! There's nothing sweeter for a crow than a man's eyeballs.

The car was lumbering along and Emmanuel sat smiling between Aubertin and myself. He seemed to understand what Cotnoir was saying. We thought the Doctor had grown into a bizarre, disturbing man. Up to then, Cotnoir had scowled but coming off the bridge he broke out, so to speak, and began to be very talkative. I didn't know he had it in him. He was extremely lucid. You encounter that in terminal cases, far gone and writing their will.

He said, ''I must speak about this in the presence of my wife. She has a large copybook. She writes down what I say. I haven't spoken to her about the crows yet. Or, at least I've stopped talking to her about them ever since they've scared me. She might think I was sick. That would make her feel bad. She has no one but me on this earth. Our house in Longueuil is the convent where she took holy orders, alone. I never was her husband. I'm a lay brother to her. Every day I go shopping and she lives off what I bring back. Out of it she makes up a world of her own. Is she happy with it? I keep her up to date but I do it my way. Then she chips in. What a strange world it must be. But it'll win out against the other one, the real one which doesn't last, which is always being created and destroyed, swallowed up in universal indifference. I sometimes tell myself she is building an ark, an ark already floating on the flood in which we are all splashing around, just about drowning in it. I've made many people climb into the ark as well as all the animals I've met during the last twenty years all over the suburbs: the last horses and the goats of that old Italian woman, stowaway roosters, dogs without a licence, parrots — very old and only able to understand English — and that beautiful deer I saw one morning, in autumn, the deer which was looking out towards Montreal and didn't understand what it was. They'll all be saved. And so will you, Emmanuel. And so will you, Aubertin, along with your wife

72

and six daughters *and* the parakeets. And so will I, of course. But I don't know if I'll recognize myself. What does my wife think of me? I haven't asked her. Still, I'd like to know. Later, when I retire, before I die, I'll read her book. My whole life is in there, day by day. I'll read it and judge myself before the good God does. Aubertin, tell me now, what do you think of me?''

Aubertin hesitated, then claimed that he couldn't say and added:

"I've never been treated by another doctor. I guess that means I think you're competent.''

"It means above all that when you were sick you weren't complacent about it and you knew I agreed. Anyway, you didn't have much choice. Who else would have gone to your house, the house of a jealous man, a savage, a five-minute walk away from the road? I liked to walk along the field full of bulrushes, especially in the fall and to think of Viger, the patriots, the *gentlemen* who for a year, one year out of two hundred, one rare, fine year became jailbirds. I also thought I'd have been in it with them. And what a tale that was. Nothing to it. Today I wouldn't be such an ass. I'd just stick to those lovely, brown, darkening bulrushes. The Patriots ended up as celebrities, you see, but the swindlers, thugs, run-of-the-mill boys who hang, don't work at this sort of thing once every two hundred years. They're at it every single day, year in, year out. Nobody thinks they've got guts. They're public enemies. That just might be a real honour. Anyway, today I think I'd simply be on their side. In fact, I always have been.''

Cotnoir added:

''I've fought my own private war too, you know.''

We were at Jean Talon station. We got the tickets, went through the tunnel, came up on the platform and the night train pulled in. The locomotive was warming up and smoked like a foundry. Steam jets hissed under the cars. We let our minds wander for a second and Emmanuel who was on the lookout for exactly that took off and ran down the platform along the standing train, his nice cap rolling against the tracks. Aubertin bent down to pick it up while Emmanuel vanished in front of the locomotive. Maybe he wanted to get to Québec on his own. The train left. Then we saw our runaway walking in the opposite direction. He had gone round the locomotive and run back on the other side of the train. He was heading for Montreal now. When the train had moved off, he stopped and turned towards us. The CPR security guard began to holler at him in a senseless dialect — English I guess. Cotnoir ran towards the station and stopped to give us hell which we could have done without. He shook his fist at us for a while. The guard walked towards him and Emmanuel vanished in the night.

When we went back to the car it wasn't where we had parked it. Cotnoir hadn't waited for us. It was late.

"Well, I'm getting up at six tomorrow," Aubertin said. He was cross. I paid for his taxi ride and didn't get home until the early dawn. Above the city the crows brought their meeting to an end with brief cries.

The day before Cotnoir had come to pick me up, to drive over to Aubertin's place and from there take Emmanuel to the station. I told him I thought his eyes looked strange. Keen. Shifty. He pretended he was suffering from indigestion. He put his unsteady hand against his chest again and again, unable to alleviate the pain and then went into a tavern in Longueuil. I didn't have to go in with him. Anyway I would have felt awkward about doing it. At the time, it was a teetotaler suburb where parish priests built their churches without paying real estate taxes. Religion seemed to be in a precarious position. They worried over it, didn't want to make it a liability and the state which dreaded subversion for some reason or other helped them out. They would settle for yearly contributions and what the collection plate raked in but they'd say: "No real estate tax! And no taverns!" so that Longueuil which must have had four entertained the whole suburb. The taverns became foreign enclaves.

By stepping in, a local resident, especially a distinguished one, ran the risk of being discredited.

Cotnoir came back to the car less shaky but still sick. He didn't worry over it too much. He was used to putting up with the ailments which he brought upon himself. He didn't imagine anything else could breed them. Like a majority of people he thought his health, like most things, was subject to his will. Drinking covered up his old age. Death already hemmed him in without his suspecting it. He had thought about dying, but in his own way, in his own good time. This doctor who had seen more invalids than happy, healthy people barely believed in illness and, so close to death himself, still could only imagine it as a kind of suicide. He had few illusions about an art whose inadequacies didn't escape him. On the other hand, it got Cotnoir over his apprehensions about himself and it was about himself that he was deluded. Still, when we had driven along the nameless street up to the Aubertin home, he sat in the car, scowling, and sent me in instead.

I was walking towards the front door. The frogs' crooning overran the darkness and rose up to the white stars. Cotnoir shouted at me through the car's open window:

"Go around the house. The door's blocked up."

"There's no dog?" I asked.

He didn't answer me and shut the car window. I felt I had asked a silly question and he hadn't thought much of me. Sure enough when we were at the station he told me suddenly, probably to ease the pain which was still making things difficult for him:

"Doctor, when dogs scare the shit out of a man he should become an oculist."

I think he put physical courage above everything else, like a really wild man, a thug, a man of honour would. His kind of medicine was always hazardous. He was the only man who would have thought of putting Emmanuel on the train leaving for Québec as therapy.

I had walked around the house between dry land and the swamp. The water was very near. I wasn't thinking about the dog any more, just trying not to step into a hole. Coming to the stairway put an end to my worries. Feeling good, I climbed up the stairs and then, very near to where I stood, on the floor of the landing the dog's tail began to beat. He was happy and was I ever! I knocked. Through the door-window I saw a woman wiping her hands on her apron and coming over to answer. I thought she must be Mrs. Aubertin, introduced myself and she said:

"But why didn't you come in through the front door?"

"I thought it was blocked up."

"It isn't any more," she said almost cheerfully. "My husband opened it tonight."

About this housewife for whom the day, whatever the catastrophe or the celebration, always ended with lots of soapy water because she had to clean up for the next day, young girls came into sight. They were more or less tall, more or less fully developed, doing nothing and putting on airs. They found security in numbers and stared me down fearlessly. I said hello to them. Some looked the other way and giggled. They probably thought Emmanuel and I were two of a kind and found me pompous.

"Won't you go into the living-room?" the mother said. "My husband's waiting for you."

Under a huge and rather seedy looking moose's head which didn't make the hunter look any younger, two men sat ramrod stiff like country bumpkins on a streetcar. One of them was getting impatient.

"I was wondering if you'd get here at all," he said. The other one sat still, smiling blissfully, rarin' to fly off like that to the far-flung ends of the earth. The young girls had followed me. They stood round a cage full of parakeets. I would have loved to sit under the moose's head and enjoy the artless, heady blend of titties, wings and beaks, thighs, sighs and teasing, but Aubertin stood up. He grabbed Emmanuel's arm and I did too. Emmanuel got up without batting an eye. He kept on smiling at — I don't know — a fixed point in space, always ahead of him whether he was standing or sitting, in the house surrounded by swampland, in Cotnoir's car or in the station. He was entranced and let us escort him. I guess it was a put-on because the muscles of his arm were still tense. I could feel them twitch, contracting and relaxing, exercising, alert. Aubertin had the same hunch.

"No fooling around now, Emmanuel," he said with his booming voice. We were leaving when the neighbour came in, bringing a cap.

"Look, Emmanuel, it's a policeman's cap. With that you can get by anywhere."

But the cap was too large. It sank down on his ears and didn't improve the sight of a man who was already befuddled.

"Hey, that's a perfect fit, that is."

"Sure," Emmanuel said.

"You'll bring it back, won't you?" said the neighbour. "That's my husband's cap."

Emmanuel looked up. He wasn't smiling any more. He was panicking.

"Boss, can I go to the can?"

"To lock himself up," thought the neighbour.

"No, you just wait and do it at the station," Aubertin answered.

Emmanuel didn't plead with him. He kept on smiling and let himself be marched off. Mrs. Aubertin then ran up, wiping her hands on her apron. She also had a hat to offer.

"Your hat, Aubertin." The municipal councillor's hat which a young girl brought to her father. And why not the moose's antlers? I felt very young and free because I was bare-headed. Between the dry ground and the swamp, the flight of steps jutted out like a wharf. The young girls' hair was light and the night was full of the frogs' croaking song. The door which had been blocked up by winter was again opening out on spring.

"Emmanuel will be saved."

"You think so?" said the neighbour.

"I'm sure he will be," Mrs. Aubertin answered.

The big sedan had driven off towards Chambly Road. The stars came back in the night sky. The girls and both women stayed a little on the wharf. Then the slight chill of a fine April night made them go back in.

Emmanuel was walking more slowly now. He was no longer stepping over every second tie. He shortened his stride, stepped from one to the other, following the railroad tracks without knowing where he was headed. Sometimes the tracks doubled, tripled, multiplied to the point where you could no longer count them. He went down junctions walking between the brightest, the glossiest tracks. He walked with lowered head in the dark corridor, not paying attention to the lights of the city or the stars. Suddenly the tracks began to quake. A beam of light caught him.

He was blinded. He wanted to run for it, but in the opposite direction another spotlight was coming at him. From his blinded eyes a shrill din welled up into his brain. The trains met and passed each other. All hell broke loose and Emmanuel felt the warm breath of both machines. The hundred windows of the cars interspaced by shadowy strips blinked on either side of him. Then darkness again and two red tail lights receding. Emmanuel was still surrounded with steam and the haze was dispelled. He caught sight of the flickering lights of the city and the sky. Confusion had vanished from his mind. A kind of self-reliance made its way within him. Among the heavenly bodies, one was his lucky star. Emmanuel saw it and no longer doubted its existence.

On the outskirts of Westmount he found some freight cars whose doors were wide open and climbed into one. The floor was littered with straw. He lay down and went to sleep. When he woke up on the next day the countryside was drifting past him like a film projection. Somebody coughed. A sturdy looking man asked him:

"You slept well?"

"Where we heading boss?"

"I'd say we're heading for Québec."

"Québec. Yeah, sure," said Emmanuel.

I saw him again some years later at a wedding reception held in the Aubertin home. He was the life of the party. Everyone tried to embarrass him and no one could. He was never at a loss for an answer. His replies were sometimes short and somewhat silly, sometimes elaborate and rather obscure. They were always swift and not very successful hints at irony. A few snappy cracks made up for others. Everyone was glad to have some good cheap fun. Only a few sober young men were disturbed by the fact that a moron had more of a sense of humour than they did. I suggested that someone ask him whether he remembered the train for Québec. Emmanuel figured out whose query it was and answered:

"The train for Québec? I 'dunno. I only take the train going to Montreal."

"And when you are in Montreal?"

"I take the train for Trois-Rivières."

"Once in Trois-Rivières?"

"The train for Batiscan, what else?"

"And in Batiscan?"

"I ride on to Grondines."

"Then, you never ride in a train bound for Québec?"

"How could I know where the train's heading? I always get off in Lorette. The train goes on wherever it wants to. That just might be Québec but I think that after a weekend in Montreal it probably goes and confesses its sins in Ste. Anne de Beaupré."

Someone wanted to know why he was always

getting off in Lorette. The reason was simple. His employer's home was there.

"That's where he hangs out when he isn't up at his logging camps."

"Where do you go when he is at the camps, Emmanuel?"

"I'm up there too. I stay put and pretend I'm working. Barely," Emmanuel added, "but I put my heart and soul into doing that."

Everyone broke out saying that he was a lucky man indeed. He agreed. Did he then catch sight of his star behind the train smoke again?

"I've always been lucky because I found out I was," he said. And turning towards me, he greeted me very politely. I went towards him to shake his hand. He turned away. I put my hand into my pocket, more satisfied with him than with myself. What more did we have to say to each other? I danced with Linda; then, claiming that a little old lady was dying or that a child was being born I went away, feeling as contented as a man can be. I hadn't betrayed Mrs. Cotnoir.

In church she had sat in the middle of a large area of empty pews between the local extras and ourselves and she seemed indescribably lonely. I felt really sorry for her but I was too old to mope over the whole thing. I was gradually getting as angry as all hell. Meanwhile the choir broke into the *Dies Irae* so feebly it seemed they were absent-minded or didn't understand a word of Latin. They weren't singing out, they were humming and lending an ear to the echo of their own voices. It was going to be a day of wrath all right but mine wasn't that of the hymn — a temper-tantrum born of a good soul's fear and swallowed up by dullness. It was the anger of a young man fit to face the wrath of God, a rage which made me rise up, full of hate and contempt for the liturgy, the priest, for Le Royer who was a conceited ass, for the notary — a swindler whose clattering plates exasperated me — for Bezeau, the undertakers, the choir and the *Dies Irae*. It was amazing. I guess it must have been caused by something deeper than the outrage of which I thought Mrs. Cotnoir the victim.

When it was time to sign the register the tall undertaker came to escort Mrs. Cotnoir. Gérin signaled to me to go along with her. I took her arm with a pride and joy I haven't felt since. We went into the vestry, The parish priest, his Eminence Cardinal Vachon came to meet us. His face was emaciated and delicate and he looked like a saint. Perhaps he was one. He bowed before Mrs. Cotnoir, took my place and escorted her to the register. Following them I thought I heard him saying to her with a peculiarly ecclesiastic magniloquence that her husband had been a great man. Cotnoir a great man. Did he really think that? Could be. In any case, Mrs. Cotnoir never doubted it.

"Mankind is shortsighted," the prelate said.

"Here we go," I thought. "Mankind's to blame and mankind will again be the springboard of his Eminence. Mankind is shortsighted, God's far-sighted and God is a prelate, what else."

I have always found the clerical steel-trap mind disagreeable. It betrays so little of the spirit. But to my surprise the old parish priest didn't labour the point. He was so sober and so polite that no matter how cross I had felt I couldn't help being pleased.

The service then seemed less hateful to me. Moreover when we came back from the vestry it was coming to an end. The priest left the altar to go and have his breakfast. The tall undertaker pulled on the church truck and began to push it towards the door. Sure enough, Bessette stood beside Le Royer. Gérin waited for Sauviat and the notary to declare that he would help them settle the matter of the estate. Sauviat was delighted and the notary was somewhat less so. Gérin wasn't too happy about Mrs. Cotnoir's return to France. He wasn't thinking about stopping her from doing it but this departure brought home to him the vulgarity of a land he loved.

We emerged from the church into the sun. There were some bystanders on the other side of the street. Suddenly I saw a kind of stiff-kneed and flappy-eared nut with a toque stuck on the back of his head, striding around in a broad, duck walk. It was really funny. On his shoulder he carried a bag which must have contained the wealth of the universe. In any case, his face expressed a feeling of tremendous satisfaction. Since the death of her husband, Mrs. Cotnoir had been continuously enquiring after Emmanuel. I said to her:

"Look, it's Emmanuel."

The strange man didn't stop. He didn't care for mourning and hearses and undertakers. He kept on going, turned on the Chambly Road and vanished. But when we were in the cemetery, standing before the black grave, just who do you think we saw? We saw him, as happy, as extraordinarily happy as ever, tramping across the cemetery and stepping all over the graves. He walked near to where we were, dazzled by the sunlight, and didn't even notice us.